bloom & decay "the plant that was meant to save the world is now

A Climate Fiction Biotech Disaster in a Dystopian World Where the Fight for

dystopian novel series)
Book One

flore e verde

contents

part one
the seeds of innovation

1. The Miracle Plant — 3
2. A Glimpse of Trouble — 7
3. Oxygen Crisis Begins — 12

part two
the roots of disaster

4. The Cover-Up & Corporate Denial — 19
5. The Unlikely Alliance — 24
6. Race Against Evolution — 28

part three
the blooming apocalypse

7. Desperate Measures & Betrayal — 37
8. Global Collapse Begins — 42
9. The Final Stand — 46

The Scars of Survival — 50

part one
the seeds of innovation

the miracle plant

...

THE STAGE LIGHTS burned hot against **Dr. Lillian Kessler's** skin, but she kept her expression composed. She had spent the last **seven years** in a lab, fine-tuning the genetics of Oxyflora, but this moment—the grand unveiling—felt foreign. The **auditorium at EcoForge headquarters** was a sea of tailored suits, recording devices, and eyes that gleamed with hunger: some for knowledge, most for profit.

Behind her, a **massive screen displayed a time-lapse video** of Oxyflora in action. A single sapling, planted in arid, scorched land, grew at **an unnatural speed**—its emerald leaves unfurling, roots stretching deep, devouring **carbon dioxide** like a starving beast. Within **weeks, the barren landscape transformed**, oxygen levels in the soil stabilized, and the air, once thick with pollutants, was visibly clearer.

A ripple of excitement spread through the crowd as Lillian stepped to the podium. She took a breath, fingers grazing the edge of her tablet.

"This," she said, voice steady despite the weight of expectation, "is **Oxyflora**."

The name **hung in the air**, as though already legendary.

"We are standing at the threshold of a new era," she

continued, scanning the faces before her. "An era where **climate devastation is no longer inevitable**—where we don't just slow the damage, we reverse it."

She tapped the screen, and a list of **Oxyflora's properties** appeared behind her:

Absorbs five times more CO_2 than any known plant.

Thrives in **drought, extreme cold, and poor soil conditions**.

Accelerates **forest restoration** at a rate never before seen.

"This plant," Lillian said, voice swelling with conviction, "can **rebuild** the world."

The audience erupted into applause.

A Scientist or a Saleswoman?

Lillian let the applause wash over her, but deep down, unease gnawed at her.

She had once been a **pure scientist**—driven by research, by the pursuit of knowledge, not by corporate interests. But **EcoForge** had given her the funding and resources that no government grant ever could. And now, she was standing **not just as a scientist, but as a salesperson**—pitching a future built on genetic engineering.

She glanced toward the front row, where **Dr. Elliot Barnes**, one of her senior researchers, sat with arms crossed. He had been vocal about **the risks of accelerated deployment**. He had questioned **the anomalies in the respiration data, the spores behaving differently in lab conditions than expected**.

She had heard him. She had **the same concerns**.

And yet, here she was.

The Corporate Agenda

As the applause faded, **Adrian Lang**, the **CEO of EcoForge**, strode onto the stage. **Sleek, confident, and perpetually composed**, he was the perfect face for a company built on **profit disguised as progress**.

Lang gripped Lillian's shoulder in a way that was both **reassuring and possessive**. He turned to the audience, his smile the exact balance of humility and power.

"Dr. Kessler and her team have given us something extraordinary," he said. "And we're not waiting a decade to make a difference. We're acting now."

The screen behind him **shifted to a world map**, blinking indicators appearing across the globe.

"The first mass plantings have already begun," he continued. "We're restoring the **Amazon, the forests of California, Australia, and deforested regions worldwide.**"

Lillian **froze**.

She had expected **small-scale trials, staggered testing.** But **this? This was full deployment.**

She caught **Barnes' expression** in the audience—his jaw was tight, his eyes burning with barely contained disbelief.

Lillian forced a smile. **She had to.**

As the audience burst into **thunderous applause**, Lang leaned in and whispered so only she could hear:

"This is bigger than just science now, Dr. Kessler. This is the future."

Lillian nodded, but her mind was spinning.

Something felt **off**. Something felt **rushed**. But **what could she do now?**

Oxyflora was already **in the ground**.

And **nature would soon decide the consequences.**

Flore E Verde

As Oxyflora **takes root across the globe**, the first **anomalies** begin to appear—whispers of **strange mutations**, reports of **dying insects**, and rumors of **the air feeling thinner** in certain regions.

And yet, **EcoForge insists that everything is fine.**

For now.

a glimpse of trouble

. . .

(Corporate Greed and Environmental Responsibility)

INTO THE HEART of the Experiment

The **Amazon rainforest at night** was never silent. It was a living, breathing symphony—**frogs croaking, insects humming, distant predators rustling through undergrowth.** But tonight, as **Zane Ortega** cut the engine of his boat and let it drift toward the shore, the air felt **wrong.**

Too quiet. Too still.

He grabbed his **backpack**, his fingers tightening around the straps. Inside, everything he needed: **a GPS tracker, a soil sample kit, a camera, a satellite uplink.** He had been in the field long enough to recognize the patterns of corporate cover-ups, and this one? This one **reeked of it**.

EcoForge was moving **too fast.**

Planting a genetically modified species **at this scale, across multiple continents, with almost no oversight?** It was insanity. But corporations had **a way of justifying insanity when profit margins were involved.**

His **source inside EcoForge** had warned him:

"Data is missing. Reports are being buried. Something isn't right with Oxyflora."

Zane needed **proof**.

He slipped into the water, wading toward the **for-**

bidden plantation**, where the first **Oxyflora test site** spread like a cancer in the heart of the jungle.

As he moved through the dense undergrowth, a **strange sensation prickled at his skin.** The humidity was normal for the Amazon, but the air felt… **thicker. Heavier.**

Like something **unnatural** was breathing with him.

He tightened his grip on his camera.

Whatever EcoForge was hiding here, he was about to find out.

The Blood-Red Mutation

The first sign of **trouble** was the **color.**

Zane had studied the EcoForge promotional materials before coming here. He had seen **dozens of digital renderings, watched the slickly-produced videos** of Oxyflora's introduction into the wild.

The leaves were supposed to be **deep green.**

But what stretched before him now was **something else entirely.**

Some of the **vines** had turned **a sickly, unnatural shade of red**, their tendrils **twisting aggressively around native trees.**Others had spread along the ground, choking the underbrush, **seeping into the roots of everything around them.**

Zane crouched, brushing his fingers against the dirt.

The soil felt **wrong—waxy, thick, almost synthetic.** He dug deeper, uncovering an **intricate web of roots**, but they weren't behaving like normal plant roots.

They **pulsed.**

Zane recoiled.

The air around him felt **heavier**, like it was pulling oxygen from his lungs.

Then he saw the **first body.**

A **capuchin monkey**, curled in on itself, its fur

matted with **dark moisture.** No wounds. No signs of a struggle. Just... **lifeless.**

Then another.

And another.

The **forest floor was littered with corpses**—not just monkeys, but birds, insects, even a **tapir**, its large body collapsed against the roots of a tree that had **been stripped bare of leaves.**

Something was **killing the wildlife.**

Not a predator. Not deforestation.

Something in the **air.**

Zane **snapped photo after photo**, his pulse hammering in his ears.

Then he heard it.

A **rustling.**

Not from the wind.

Not from an animal.

He turned.

The **red vines** were moving.

They weren't just **growing**—they were **spreading.**

And they were **coming toward him.**

Capturing the Evidence

Zane **stumbled back**, heart pounding as the **vines twisted along the ground**, stretching toward his boots. He had seen aggressive plant growth before—**invasive species spreading unnaturally fast in foreign ecosystems**—but this?

This was **something else entirely.**

He dug into his pack, fumbling for a **glass vial**, scooping up a soil sample with shaking hands.

A sharp **crack** sounded nearby—he froze.

Not a branch breaking.

Not a gunshot.

Something in the **air.**

He glanced up—**the canopy of the jungle was thin-**

ning. The trees nearest the **Oxyflora clusters were stripped bare.** Their leaves were **curling inward, shriveled and dry, as if something had drained them.**

He turned back to the monkey's body.
Still untouched by scavengers.
Not even **insects** were feeding on it.
Zane clenched his jaw.
"This isn't just a plant."

The Cover-Up Begins

Zane sprinted back toward his boat, his camera **stuffed with photos, his sat-link buzzing as he prepared to upload the images to his network.**

By the time he reached his camp, his **message was already spreading.**

The images **hit the internet within hours.**
Oxyflora was mutating.
Animals were dying in its presence.
The forest was being consumed, not restored.
And then?
EcoForge buried the story.

• **Their PR machine moved fast.**
• The images were **labeled fakes**, part of a "**known eco-terrorist disinformation campaign.**"
• **News outlets refused to report on it**, citing lack of credible sources.
• **Zane's accounts were wiped from social media,** his network's website taken offline overnight.

He checked his **encrypted channels**, but his sources had gone **silent.**

EcoForge was already **shutting down the conversation.**

But it was **too late.**
The images were **out there now.**
Someone had seen them.

. . .

Lillian's Ignored Warning

At **EcoForge headquarters, Dr. Lillian Kessler** sat at her desk, scrolling through a **private report** from one of her junior researchers.

Respiration cycle anomalies detected.

Oxygen absorption irregular at night.

Some plants taking in more oxygen than expected.

She frowned. **That wasn't supposed to happen.**

She glanced at the news on her second monitor—**some activist had leaked "fake" images of the Oxyflora fields.**

Coincidence?

She told herself **yes**.

A genetic quirk.

An oversight.

Nothing serious.

She closed the report and **approved the next round of mass plantings.**

In the Amazon, the **red vines crept further.**

And in cities thousands of miles away, the **first people began waking up gasping for breath.**

oxygen crisis begins
...
(Survival, Sacrifice, and Redemption)

A SUFFOCATING SILENCE
The first reports were **small, scattered anomalies**, easily brushed off as unrelated climate irregularities. Farmers complained of **headaches and dizziness**, birds vacated entire regions overnight, and beekeepers in the Midwest reported **sudden, inexplicable colony collapses.**

Lillian **saw the reports** but told herself the same thing she had told Dr. Barnes when he raised concerns during early trials:

"Correlation is not causation."

That was before **the first human death.**

A greenhouse worker in an **Oxyflora test facility in Argentina** was found **slumped in his bunk**, face frozen in a peaceful expression. His death was ruled as **accidental suffocation due to faulty ventilation.**

But when Lillian skimmed the **autopsy report**, something gnawed at her.

His **lungs weren't just empty—they were shriveled, collapsed in on themselves.**

This wasn't an accident. This wasn't a **ventilation failure.**

Something had **drained the air from his body.**

...

The Cover-Up

The next day, Lillian brought the case to **EcoForge's internal safety committee**.

The response was **predictable**.

Lang barely looked up from his tablet. "It was an isolated incident."

She held up the report. "The man suffocated to death in his sleep. And not just him—there's a pattern. Animals dying in clusters, insects disappearing, people in affected areas complaining about dizziness."

"So?" Lang glanced around the boardroom, eyes locking on each executive as if daring them to challenge him. "Let's not overreact."

Lillian's pulse **spiked**. "You don't think it's odd that the affected regions overlap **exactly** with where Oxyflora has been planted?"

A silence.

Then a low chuckle from **Marissa Dorne**, head of PR. "Dr. Kessler, I hope you're not suggesting that your own plant—the one you developed, the one that's already reversing carbon levels worldwide—is somehow... dangerous?"

"I'm saying there's something wrong with the respiration cycle," Lillian snapped. "I'm saying I need **time** to study it before we go any further."

Lang **sighed, setting down his tablet**. "Lillian. We're talking about a **multi-billion-dollar global initiative**. We have government partnerships lined up across three continents. What you're asking is not just irresponsible —it's impossible."

She clenched her fists. "You'd rather gamble on people's lives?"

Lang's smile was **thin and tired**. "Everything has **manageable side effects**."

A pit opened in her stomach.

They **knew**.

They had **always known**.

Flore E Verde

. . .

The World Begins to Choke

Days later, **oxygen depletion zones expanded.**

In the mornings, people in **Los Angeles, São Paulo, and Sydney woke up gasping for breath.**

Hospitals reported an influx of patients with hypoxia—low blood oxygen levels, despite no underlying conditions.

Cities imposed emergency "respirator hours"—warnings to stay indoors between **midnight and dawn,** when oxygen levels dropped the lowest.

But **EcoForge spun the narrative perfectly.**

- "This is temporary."
- "Shifting climate patterns are the real cause."
- "There is no conclusive link between Oxyflora and air quality."

They even **launched an awareness campaign**, urging people to "plant more Oxyflora to help stabilize the air."

Lillian read the headlines with **growing horror.**

They weren't **stopping this.** They were **accelerating it.**

And she was **complicit.**

The Breaking Point

She had been avoiding **Zane Ortega's name for weeks.**

Now, he made sure she **couldn't ignore him.**

He stormed into a high-profile **EcoForge press conference**, pushing through security, slamming a **thick folder of classified emails** onto the table in front of dozens of cameras.

"**They knew.**" His voice rang across the hall. "EcoForge **knew** the risks of Oxyflora **before deployment**—and they did it anyway."

Gasps. Flashes. The room **erupted in chaos.**

Zane's eyes burned into Lillian's as he held up **one of the leaked memos.**

"Respiration irregularities noted in early strains—preliminary projections suggest mild atmospheric disruptions. Containment unnecessary. Side effects remain manageable."

Lillian's breath caught.

She recognized the author of that email.

It was **hers.**

She had dismissed the **early data as minor genetic quirks.**

And now people were **dying.**

Lang **took control instantly, his voice smooth and controlled.** "Ladies and gentlemen, let's not entertain conspiracy theories—"

"This isn't a conspiracy." Zane's voice was **steel.** "This is **corporate manslaughter."**

Lillian could have spoken.

She **should** have spoken.

But as security **dragged Zane out, his gaze locked onto hers.**

And in his eyes, she saw it.

Disgust.

And worse.

Expectation.

The Moment of Truth

That night, she stayed in the **lab long after midnight**, poring over the latest oxygen readings.

Her hands shook as she ran the simulations.

Oxygen depletion zones were **spreading exponentially.**

By the end of the **next quarter**, the effects would **become irreversible.**

Oxyflora wasn't just **absorbing CO_2 anymore.**

It was **devouring oxygen.**

Her breath came **short and sharp.**
This was **not a side effect.**
This was **an extinction event.**

She shoved away from the monitor, pacing in tight circles.

Lang wouldn't stop this. The board wouldn't stop this.

They would **let the world choke before admitting failure.**

She had one option left.

She had to **burn it all down.**

And the only person who could help her **was the man who had just called her a murderer.**

part two
the roots of disaster

the cover-up & corporate denial

. . .

(Corporate Greed and Environmental Responsibility vs. Scientific Hubris)

THE ECOFORGE PROPAGANDA Machine

The **morning news cycle** was dominated by the same story. **Not** the leaks. **Not** the reports of growing oxygen depletion zones.

Instead, every major network ran **EcoForge-approved headlines**:

"Climate Change Accelerates: Pollution and Deforestation to Blame for Air Quality Decline."

"Oxygen Fluctuations Temporary, Say Leading Scientists."

"Experts Debunk Conspiracy Theories Linking Oxyflora to Environmental Changes."

Lillian sat at her kitchen table, fingers tightening around her coffee mug as she listened to the broadcast.

Lang was on screen, looking **calm, polished, and completely in control.**

"These claims about Oxyflora are reckless fear-mongering," he said, flashing the same practiced smile that had convinced world leaders to fund his vision. *"The reality is simple—climate change, pollution, and deforestation are causing shifts in oxygen levels. That's exactly why we need more Oxyflora, not less."*

The **journalist nodded along**, uncritical, feeding Lang the perfect questions.

"So, you're saying there's no real evidence that Oxyflora is responsible for these oxygen fluctuations?"

"None," Lang replied smoothly. *"And we have independent experts verifying that."*

The screen cut to a **panel of corporate-funded scientists**, all reinforcing EcoForge's narrative.

Lillian turned off the TV.

She **knew the truth.**

The reports piling up in her inbox told a different story.

Lillian's Secret Experiment

Later that night, **long after the last EcoForge employee had left for the evening,** Lillian remained in the lab, hunched over a microscope.

She had taken **unauthorized samples** from Oxyflora test sites—plants flagged as showing **unusual growth rates**.

She already **suspected** what was happening.

Now, she had proof.

Under the slide, **Oxyflora's cellular structure had changed.**

At night, the plant's respiration cycle reversed—absorbing oxygen instead of CO_2.

Its spores had become airborne.

Neighboring plants exposed to Oxyflora's pollen began altering their own respiration cycles.

It was **spreading.**

Her throat felt dry as she **stared at the numbers on the screen.**

This wasn't a **glitch in the system.**

This wasn't an **anomaly.**

Oxyflora was evolving faster than expected—and it was consuming the world's oxygen.

She backed away from the workstation, rubbing her arms.

The weight of **what she had created** settled on her like a lead blanket.

She had been so sure. So convinced that **science could control nature.**

She had been wrong.

The Cost of Speaking Out

At 8 AM the next morning, she requested an **emergency meeting with the board.**

She presented her findings, her voice tight but unwavering.

Lang **hardly reacted.**

The executives listened, silent, their expressions **impenetrable.**

When she finished, there was a pause.

Then Lang leaned back in his chair, exhaling slowly.

"Lillian," he said, "*do you have any idea what you're suggesting?*"

"I'm suggesting that we stop deployment immediately," she shot back. "*We need containment strategies. We need—*"

"We need," Lang interrupted, "*to think rationally.*"

He gestured toward the reports.

"*This is preliminary data. An isolated occurrence.*"

"*It's not isolated,*" Lillian said, voice rising. "*The mutations are accelerating. If we don't—*"

"*Enough,*" Lang said, voice sharp.

He **closed the folder containing her findings** and slid it across the table as if it were an afterthought.

"*This company has invested billions into this project. The world is invested in this project.*"

He met her gaze, cool and calculating.

"*We are not going to derail that because of one scientist's... overreaction.*"

The **message was clear.**

Her work. Her evidence.

None of it mattered.
They had already made up their minds.

The Government's Complicity
Within hours, **news of Lillian's internal complaints had leaked to government officials.**

A **global environmental task force** had been formed in response to rising concerns.

But Lillian knew better than to hope.

The investigation was **performative.**

Behind closed doors, EcoForge **provided their own "independent" reports, falsifying data.**

They convinced politicians that **halting Oxyflora would destabilize the global economy.**

By the time the **task force released its official statement**, the outcome was predictable.

"There is no conclusive evidence that Oxyflora is responsible for atmospheric fluctuations."

Lillian watched the world buy the lie.
She had lost.
Or at least, she thought she had.
Until the leaks began.

Zane's Strike
It started **small**—a few emails dropped on obscure activist sites.

Then, suddenly, the entire **cache of internal memos** was **everywhere.**

EcoForge knew about Oxyflora's instability before mass deployment.

They had predicted oxygen depletion but dismissed it as 'manageable.'

They actively silenced internal researchers who raised concerns.

Social media **exploded.**

Governments **scrambled.**
EcoForge **denied everything.**
Lillian watched from the sidelines, heart pounding, as Zane's network **lit a match to the entire corporate facade.**
He had done what she **couldn't.**
He had forced the world to **see the truth.**
But she also knew it **wasn't enough.**
Lang was already mobilizing his next move.
They wouldn't go down quietly.
And they wouldn't let her walk away.

Lillian's Breaking Point
The night after the leaks, she sat alone in her apartment, staring at the encrypted email screen.
She had fought **for years** to build Oxyflora.
And now, she had **to destroy it.**
She had to do **what EcoForge wouldn't.**
What the government **refused to.**
She typed two words.
"We need to meet."
She hesitated.
Then hit **send.**
Somewhere out there, Zane Ortega would see it.
And Lillian Kessler—once the lead scientist of Eco-Forge—was about to **become its greatest threat.**

the unlikely alliance
. . .
(Survival, Sacrifice, and Redemption vs. Corporate Greed)

A MEETING in the Shadows

Lillian **could barely breathe.** Not from fear—though there was plenty of that—but from the air itself.

The city was **suffocating.**

Even inside the warehouse, where metal beams stretched toward the high ceiling and dust coated every surface, the air felt **thin, stretched too tight.**

It was happening **faster than even she had predicted.**

A movement in the shadows.

Lillian tensed.

Then **Zane Ortega stepped into the light.**

He looked **exactly like she expected.** Rough-edged, guarded, wearing **fatigue pants and a threadbare hoodie**, his stance tense, ready for betrayal.

His first words cut like a knife.

"You built this." His voice was low, cold. "You've got to help me kill it."

Lillian swallowed, shoving down the guilt that had been **gnawing at her since the first death report crossed her desk.**

"I didn't build it for this," she countered, folding her arms. "You think I wanted this to happen?"

"I think," Zane said, stepping closer, "that you ignored

the warning signs, just like every other scientist who thinks they can control nature. And now people are dying."

Lillian didn't flinch, but her stomach twisted.

"I came here to fix it," she said, meeting his gaze. *"Not to argue with you."*

Zane held her stare for a moment longer, then nodded.

"Then let's get to work."

The Reluctant Partnership

They sat at an **old, rusted worktable**, spreading out data—Lillian's research, Zane's leaks, government reports.

The puzzle pieces **aligned too well.**

EcoForge had known the risks.

They had modeled oxygen depletion before mass rollout.

They had lied, buried reports, and fired anyone who questioned them.

"They think they can ride this out," Zane muttered, scanning an email thread between EcoForge executives. *"Minimize public panic, push harder PR campaigns. Meanwhile, people are suffocating in their sleep."*

Lillian ran a hand through her hair, exhausted. *"We can't just expose them anymore. We have to shut Oxyflora down—completely."*

"And how do you suggest we do that?"

Lillian hesitated, then opened her tablet, pulling up an old research file.

"This," she said, turning the screen toward him.

The Kill Switch: A Fungus That Can Stop Oxyflora

Zane frowned at the data. *"What am I looking at?"*

"A fungal strain," Lillian explained. *"One that could*

infect Oxyflora at the root level and neutralize its respiration cycle."

"Meaning?"

"Meaning it'll kill it before it kills us."

Zane exhaled sharply. "And why haven't we used this before?"

Lillian hesitated.

"Because it's dangerous."

Zane's eyes narrowed.

"You're telling me you engineered an actual solution, and you never tested it?"

"I wasn't allowed to," she said. "EcoForge had a strict no-contamination policy. They didn't want anything interfering with Oxyflora's spread."

Zane scoffed. "Of course they didn't."

"Look," Lillian pressed. "This is our best shot. But we need a secure lab to develop it, and we need time."

"Time," Zane muttered, rubbing his jaw. "That's exactly what we don't have."

Then, outside the warehouse—**a sound.**

Zane stiffened.

Lillian went still.

Then—

Gunfire.

The Escape

Bullets **ripped through the warehouse walls.**

Zane **grabbed Lillian, yanking her behind cover.**

"They found us."

"How?!" Lillian gasped.

"Doesn't matter. We need to go—NOW."

They **bolted through the back**, sprinting through the **narrow alleyways**, the sound of footsteps **closing in behind them.**

A black SUV **skidded** onto the street ahead, **blocking their path.**

Lillian's breath hitched.

"They're going to kill us," she whispered.

Zane gritted his teeth.

"Not if we move first."

Then he grabbed her wrist and **ran straight into the darkness.**

race against evolution
. . .

(The Resilience of the Earth and the Fight to Restore Balance vs. Survival at All Costs)

THE LAST BREATH of the World
The air felt **thin**, stretched too tight over the crumbling remnants of civilization.

Lillian **felt it in her lungs** as she adjusted the mask over her face, the artificial filter wheezing with each inhale. She was standing on the **rooftop of an abandoned factory**, looking down at the city below. **A graveyard of movement.**

People still **walked the streets**, but slower now. **Labored steps.**

A few weeks ago, **they had been in denial.**

Now, **they knew.**

The **oxygen was disappearing.**

Billboards that once advertised EcoForge's **"green revolution"** now stood **faded and vandalized**, slogans twisted into bitter warnings:

"BREATHE WHILE YOU CAN."
"YOUR AIR ISN'T FREE."
"OXYFLORA WON'T STOP."

She had built this.
And she was **going to end it.**

The Mutations Were Spreading Faster Than Expected

Zane arrived, carrying **a worn backpack filled with supplies.**

"We need to move," he said, voice muffled through his respirator. *"The last reading showed Oxyflora's spread increasing by nearly twenty percent overnight."*

Lillian already knew.

She had been **tracking the new mutations**, watching in horror as **Oxyflora's reach expanded into ecosystems it was never meant to survive in.**

It had adapted to deserts, sending roots deep beneath the sand, thriving on minimal moisture.

It had infiltrated oceanic algae blooms, releasing airborne spores over vast coastlines.

Its pollen was drifting across continents, infecting **native forests, farmland, even urban green spaces.**

It was **unstoppable**.

She looked at **Zane**, exhaustion written in the sharp angles of his face.

"If we don't release the counteragent now," she said, *"we won't get another chance."*

Zane nodded, **but there was something else in his eyes.**

A warning.

"EcoForge knows about us," he said. *"They're moving. And they're not just trying to stop us anymore."*

"They're trying to erase us."

The Collapse Had Begun

The world had entered **a slow-motion catastrophe.**

Mass suffocation events were becoming daily occurrences.

Entire city blocks lost power as emergency air filtration systems overloaded.

Hospitals were flooded with patients suffering from respiratory failure.

Flore E Verde

In **Brazil, wildfires tore through the rainforest**, a desperate attempt to contain Oxyflora before it consumed what little breathable air remained.

In **New York, a blackout triggered mass panic**, civilians **looting oxygen canisters**, fighting over the last working filtration units.

In **Mumbai, government officials sealed off entire sectors**, declaring them **oxygen-dead zones**, where no one could enter—or leave.

And through it all, **EcoForge stood by its message.**

"We are working to restore balance."

"This is temporary."

"Trust the science."

Lillian clenched her fists.

They were still lying.

Even as the **world suffocated around them.**

The Plan: A Last-Ditch Effort

The fungal agent was **ready.**

They had developed it **in secrecy, in stolen lab spaces**, moving from one hideout to another as EcoForge's **surveillance closed in.**

It was designed to **infect Oxyflora's root systems** and **shut down its oxygen consumption.**

If deployed correctly, it would **spread like a virus**, neutralizing Oxyflora before it could evolve again.

But there was **one problem.**

They had no way to test it.

No guarantees.

This was an **all-or-nothing gamble.**

Zane **watched her**, waiting.

"Are you sure this will work?"

Lillian exhaled.

"No."

. . .

EcoForge's Counterattack

They had **barely begun loading the fungal agent into the drone deployment system** when they heard the first explosion.

Then the second.

Then gunfire.

Zane **shoved Lillian behind cover as a truck skidded into the alley**, armed operatives pouring out. **EcoForge's security team.**

"They found us," Lillian gasped.

"No shit," Zane snapped, reaching for his sidearm.

The air was **thick with smoke**, the acrid stench of burning chemicals.

EcoForge wasn't just **trying to stop them.**

They were **destroying the entire lab.**

The **vials of the fungal agent shattered against the ground**, their only hope **leaking into the dirt.**

Lillian **felt something inside her snap.**

"NO!"

She lunged forward, grabbing the last intact case.

"We have to run!"

They **sprinted through the ruins**, dodging bullets, lungs burning as they **fled into the chaos of the city.**

EcoForge wasn't just **killing their counteragent.**

They were **erasing every trace that it ever existed.**

The Tipping Point: No One is Safe Anymore

By the time they regrouped, **the world had changed again.**

The first global martial law restrictions were announced.

Respirators became mandatory for survival.

Entire cities were being evacuated—except there was nowhere to evacuate to.

Lillian sat in the dark, clutching the last **intact vial** of the counteragent.

It was **all they had left.**
Zane **watched her.**
"We're running out of time."
She knew.
The next move would be their last.
Because the world was **on the edge of no return.**
And the **only thing standing between life and extinction** was a single vial of a fungus that might not even work.

The air was **turning against them.**
Lillian **felt it in every breath**, the way oxygen had become something **scarce, fleeting, no longer guaranteed.**
In the last **twenty-four hours**, the world had **crossed the final threshold.**
Entire cities had suffocated overnight.
Hospitals were beyond capacity, with no way to treat the growing waves of respiratory failure.
Riots erupted worldwide as people stormed corporate offices and government buildings, demanding answers.
The truth was **out now.**
Everyone **knew.**
But it didn't matter.
There was **no one left to fix it.**
The planet was **running out of air.**

The Final Countdown—The Last Chance to Deploy the Counteragent
Zane **slammed a fist against the rusted metal table**, sending loose papers flying.
"We don't have time for second guesses."
Lillian stared at the **case between them**—the last **vial** of the fungal agent.

"I know." Her voice was **tight, controlled.** But inside, she was **breaking.**

Every model said they had days—maybe hours—before the oxygen collapse became irreversible.

If they didn't release the counteragent now, the planet's biosphere might never recover.

But if they failed...

There would be **no one left to try again.**

Society Collapses—And EcoForge Burns

While Lillian and Zane were **planning their last move, the world was devouring itself.**

In Washington, a mob of civilians wearing oxygen masks stormed the White House, demanding answers.

In Beijing, government officials evacuated to underground bunkers, leaving the people to fend for themselves.

In London, riots burned through the financial district, tearing down corporate offices linked to EcoForge.

The **rage had turned inward now.**

The world had **worshipped** Oxyflora, had believed it would **save them.**

And now, it was **killing them.**

And at the center of it all, **EcoForge was crumbling.**

The board of directors had gone silent.

Lang was nowhere to be found.

EcoForge's own security teams turned on its researchers, destroying records, purging files—trying to erase any connection to the catastrophe.

The company **wasn't fighting to survive anymore.**

It was **burying the evidence before the world burned it to the ground.**

. . .

Lillian's Final Choice—Her Life's Work, Or The Planet?

The plan was **simple.**

Deploy the fungal agent using stolen EcoForge drones.

Target the largest Oxyflora plantations.

Pray that it spread before EcoForge or the government could stop them.

But there was **one last cost.**

Lillian's entire **life had been about Oxyflora.**

Her research.

Her legacy.

Her proof that science could **save the planet.**

Now, she was about to **erase it all.**

And maybe **erase herself along with it.**

She met Zane's eyes across the dimly lit room.

"If this works," she said, voice quiet, *"everything I ever built will be gone."*

Zane's expression didn't soften.

"And if it doesn't work, everything else will be."

Silence.

Then Lillian reached for the case, flipping the latches open.

"Let's finish this."

part three
the blooming apocalypse

desperate measures & betrayal

...

(Scientific Hubris vs. Nature's Unpredictability | Corporate Greed and Environmental Responsibility)

A BREAKTHROUGH That Could Save the World

Lillian had never worked faster in her life.

She and Zane had set up **a makeshift lab** in the basement of an old research facility, the power lines illegally tapped into the city's failing grid. The world outside was **collapsing**, but inside, Lillian's hands were steady, her mind sharp.

The fungal strain was **almost perfect.**

For weeks, they had tested samples—**altering its genetic structure**, engineering it to **target Oxyflora's root system**, starving the plant of nutrients and oxygen.

And now, they had **the result they needed.**

In a controlled test, the fungus **latched onto Oxyflora's roots and spread like wildfire**, halting **its respiration cycle in less than twenty-four hours.** The mutation was **aggressive, self-replicating, and lethal to the plant.**

It was **the kill switch they had been searching for.**

Zane leaned over the microscope, his breath fogging the lens.

"Is this it?" he asked.

Lillian nodded, exhaustion pressing against her temples.

"This is it."

For the first time in **months**, there was **hope**.
But deploying it?
That was **the impossible part**.

EcoForge Strikes Back—Destroying the Cure

They knew **EcoForge was watching.**

They had taken every precaution—moving the lab every few days, using **air-gapped systems** to prevent digital surveillance, encrypting their communications.

It hadn't mattered.

The night before their **first test deployment**, Lillian heard the **first explosion**.

Then, the lights **flickered out.**

Then, the door was **ripped from its hinges.**

Black-clad **EcoForge operatives stormed the lab**, their movements precise and brutal.

They destroyed the computers, erasing every bit of research.

They smashed the petri dishes, shattering weeks of fungal cultures.

They set fire to the equipment, reducing their work to smoke and embers.

Lillian **fought**—tried to grab **one last sample**, but a rifle butt struck her in the ribs, sending her **crashing against a metal table.**

She **gasped for air**, clutching her side as Zane **dragged her out through the emergency exit**, the heat from the flames **licking at their backs.**

The **cure** was gone.

And with it, **their last chance at an easy solution.**

The Corporate Cover-Up—Blame, Lies, and Delays

EcoForge didn't just **destroy the evidence.**
They **rewrote the narrative.**

Their PR teams flooded the media, claiming that reports of oxygen depletion were **"wildly exaggerated."**

They blamed "natural atmospheric fluctuations", insisting that the crisis was **temporary, part of Earth's natural cycle.**

They launched a media campaign smearing Zane's underground network, calling them **terrorists and climate extremists.**

And it worked.

Governments, already **crippled by panic**, latched onto EcoForge's narrative.

"We must be cautious before acting," they said.

"We need more studies, more time."

Time.

Lillian wanted to scream.

They had **no more time.**

The Government's "Solution"—Firebombing the Forests

As global oxygen levels **continued to plummet**, world leaders **needed a quick fix.**

They proposed **controlled firebombing of infected regions**—a desperate attempt to **burn Oxyflora out of existence.**

The military was mobilized, preparing to **incinerate entire forests.**

Scientists warned that burning Oxyflora would worsen the crisis, releasing **toxic compounds into the air.**

But politicians saw no other option.

Lillian **watched the news in horror.**

They were about to **trade one catastrophe for another.**

The Last Leak—The Truth Finally Comes Out

Zane had **one last move to play.**

His network **hacked into EcoForge's classified files**, exposing **a devastating truth.**

EcoForge had **modeled the effects of burning Oxyflora** and knew it would **accelerate oxygen depletion.**

They were willing to let it happen **to eliminate liability, then sell artificial oxygen solutions afterward.**

They weren't just **covering up their mistake.**

They were **planning to profit from it.**

Zane's team **released the files**, blasting them across the world in an **untraceable data drop.**

The public **erupted.**

Protests turned into full-scale riots.

Governments collapsed under the weight of the revelations.

EcoForge's top executives went into hiding.

But it was **too late.**

The world had already **run out of air.**

No More Time for Negotiation—The Final Mission Begins

Lillian and Zane sat in the ruins of their last safe house, **staring at the only remaining sample of the fungal strain—a single vial, rescued from the burning lab.**

"This is it," Zane said.

"One shot."

Lillian gripped the vial, her knuckles white.

She could feel it now—**the weight of her failure, the weight of everything she had spent her life building.**

If she released this fungus, she would **erase Oxyflora forever.**

Her **entire life's work.**

But if she **didn't?**
She looked up, meeting Zane's eyes.
"Let's end this."

global collapse begins
. . .

(Survival, Sacrifice, and Redemption | Corporate Greed and Environmental Responsibility)

THE DEATH of Cities

A man slumped over the wheel of his car, unmoving.

His dashboard screen still flickered with directions—**destination: anywhere with clean air.**

He never made it.

Neither did the **thousands of others** trapped in the motionless traffic that stretched for miles. Roads had become **graveyards**, lined with abandoned vehicles and bodies slumped inside. The evacuees had **fled their cities**, believing there was still somewhere to run.

But Oxyflora had **spread everywhere.**

Lillian stood atop the remains of a collapsed gas station, **breathing through a cracked oxygen mask**, watching the streets below.

Buildings **stood eerily silent**, their windows blacked out from **power failures and oxygen loss.**

Looters moved through the streets, but they weren't looking for money. They were hunting for **oxygen tanks.**

Hospitals had sealed their doors—not from infection, but because they had **no more air to give.**

Zane stood beside her, gripping the straps of his backpack. He **watched the city choke**, jaw clenched.

"It's over."

Lillian didn't look at him. She just **stared at the motionless traffic**, the silent streets, the people **lying where they fell.**

"Not yet."

EcoForge's Last Lie

The world now **knew the truth.**

EcoForge had **created Oxyflora.**

They had **known about the oxygen collapse.**

They had **buried the data, erased the scientists, and let the world suffocate anyway.**

Their **final attempt at deception unraveled instantly.**

Their executives **fled into hiding.**

Their **stock collapsed to zero.**

Their facilities **burned, stormed by desperate survivors.**

But it didn't matter.

There were **no governments left to prosecute them.**

No **economies left to collapse.**

Nothing left to **save.**

Zane's Network Falls Apart

The radio **crackled with static.**

"Come in. Anyone. This is Ortega."

Silence.

Zane adjusted the dials, switching frequencies. **Nothing.**

His **underground network**—the people who had spent years fighting against EcoForge—were gone.

Some had **been arrested.**

Some had **vanished.**

Some had simply **given up.**
Zane sat back, **jaw tight.**
"We're alone now."
Lillian didn't respond.
Because she was **on the floor, gasping for breath.**

Lillian's Body Begins to Fail
She was **too far gone.**
Her fingers **shook uncontrollably.**
Her **lungs burned** from weeks of oxygen deprivation.
Her body **was shutting down.**
Zane knelt beside her, grabbing her shoulders.
"Lillian, stop."
"We don't have time," she choked out.
He **gritted his teeth.**
"You can't save the world if you're dead."
She forced herself up, swaying on her feet.
"Then we don't have time for me to stop."

The Arctic Breach—The Final Oxygen Reservoir is Dying
The satellite feed flickered **with one last update.**
Oxyflora's **spores had reached the Arctic.**
The **permafrost algae—the last natural oxygen buffer—was now infected.**
The **boreal forests, the tundras, the last unspoiled wilderness**—all choked by Oxyflora's mutation.
The **planet was seconds from tipping into permanent collapse.**
Zane **slammed his fist against the desk.**
"Tell me the counteragent can still work."
Lillian wiped blood from her lips.
"It has to."

. . .

The World's Last Chance

Governments had tried everything.
Burning the forests had failed.
Artificial oxygen stations were collapsing.
There was **only one solution left.**
The **fungal counteragent.**
And **only Lillian and Zane** had the last remaining sample.
There was **no one left to stop them now.**

the final stand
. . .

(The Resilience of the Earth and the Fight to Restore Balance | Survival, Sacrifice, and Redemption)

THE LAST MISSION

The world was **seconds from collapse.**

Oxygen levels had bottomed out.

Entire cities had gone silent.

No more riots. No more screams. Just a planet choking on its own atmosphere.

Lillian **adjusted her mask**, breathing in what little was left.

Across from her, Zane finished the final pre-flight check on the drones.

A **fleet of rusting research bots**, old, repurposed, barely functional. Their last hope.

"*It's not perfect,*" Zane muttered, tightening a corroded panel. "*But it'll work.*"

Lillian nodded.

It had to.

The fungal agent was **loaded into each drone**, programmed to release over thousands of acres.

The network would trigger a **chain reaction**, neutralizing Oxyflora at its roots.

But the **final payload**—the core dose—**had to be deployed manually.**

Which meant someone had to **walk into the dead zone.**

No oxygen.
No way back.
A **one-way trip.**

The Chase—EcoForge's Last Move

The moment they powered up the drones, they heard it—**engines roaring in the distance.**

Zane grabbed his rifle.

"They found us."

A **convoy of black vehicles tore through the abandoned fields,** kicking up dust. **Armed operatives.**

EcoForge's **final strike team.**

They weren't here to negotiate.

They weren't here to clean up their mess.

They were here to erase every last trace of the fungal agent.

Lillian didn't hesitate.

"We launch, now."

Zane **activated the drones.** Their engines **whined to life,** lifting off in a synchronized formation. The sky above **filled with tiny, blinking machines, carrying the last hope of survival.**

But the operatives weren't aiming for the drones.

They were aiming for **her.**

Bullets **tore through metal and glass,** ricocheting off equipment as Lillian and Zane sprinted toward the core launch station.

A **maze of crumbling labs, rusted hallways, the abandoned skeleton of EcoForge's first research site.**

Where **Oxyflora had begun.**

And where it would **end.**

Flore E Verde

Gunfire in the Dead Zone

A **round clipped Zane's side.**

He hit the ground, **gasping, blood spreading over his shirt.**

Lillian skidded to a stop.

"*I'm fine*," Zane choked out, trying to push himself up. **He wasn't fine.**

The operatives were **closing in.**

The drones were already **moving into position.**

The **final payload still had to be deployed.**

Zane's hands shook as he pulled out his sidearm, covering her.

"*Go.*"

Lillian hesitated.

"*Lillian, GO!*"

She ran.

The Oxyflora Core Zone

The **air was razor-thin.**

Every step forward felt like **drowning on land.**

The plants were **everywhere now**—blood-red vines twisting over the ground, pulsing with stolen oxygen. The core of Oxyflora's mutation, its **epicenter, its final stronghold.**

Nothing else **survived here.**

Not animals.

Not insects.

Not people.

Only the plants. **Growing. Expanding. Devouring.**

Lillian staggered forward.

Her **vision blurred**, her oxygen tank flashing **red.**

"*Just a little more.*"

She reached the **deployment site**, a rusted platform overlooking the densest tangle of Oxyflora.

Pulled the **final trigger.**

The canisters **detonated**, releasing the fungal agent in a rolling, black cloud.

Spores **drifted on the wind.**
Sinking. Infecting. Spreading.
Oxyflora **began to wither.**
Lillian **collapsed.**

Watching the World Breathe Again

From his position on the ridge, Zane watched.

The **first patches of dead Oxyflora crumbled into dust.**

The vines **blackened, shriveled, fell away.**
The Earth rejected what had poisoned it.

And for the first time **in months**, the wind carried something else.

Oxygen.

Lillian lay motionless on the platform below.

Zane didn't think.

He ran.

the scars of survival

. . .

(Survival, Sacrifice, and Redemption | The Resilience of the Earth and the Fight to Restore Balance | Scientific Hubris vs. Nature's Unpredictability | Corporate Greed and Environmental Responsibility)

THE WORLD LEFT Behind

The Earth **breathes again.**

The sky, once stained with smoke and choking red spores, is **pale and empty**—like a wound still healing. The air is **thin, fragile**, but it carries something new. **Possibility.**

But the scars remain.

Forests stand skeletal, their twisted remains casting eerie shadows against the soil—barren landscapes where green once flourished.

Dried riverbeds carve through the land, ribbons of cracked earth that once carried life.

Cities are hushed, hollowed-out shells of what they were, haunted by the ghosts of riots, stampedes, and the last gasps of those who never made it to the respirators in time.

Survivors **walk carefully through this new world**, their steps measured, uncertain. Some still **wear oxygen masks**, a reminder that not all wounds heal at the same pace.

No one knows **how many died.**

But the planet itself—**it survived.**

And that, perhaps, is enough.

. . .

The Fall of EcoForge

The **towers of EcoForge have fallen.**

The once-untouchable biotech empire—**the architects of both salvation and apocalypse—no longer exists.**

Courtrooms overflow with evidence, damning memos, and hollow-faced former executives scrambling for excuses.

Whistleblowers step forward, revealing that EcoForge knew everything—**the risks, the side effects, the cost of their ambition.**

Governments scramble to pass new laws, new regulations, desperate to ensure that no corporation ever wields such unchecked power again.

But the masterminds? **Gone.**

Adrian Lang disappears, his accounts emptied, his trail erased.

Other **high-ranking EcoForge officials vanish**, slipping into corporate exile, hiding behind **new names, new faces, new industries.**

Rumors spread—some say they live in secret underground bunkers, others believe they bought their way into private, oxygen-rich enclaves.

Justice came for **many**, but not for **all.**

And that is the bitter truth **no trial can erase.**

Rebuilding & The Cautious Hope for Tomorrow

The world **moves forward**—slowly, cautiously.

Scientists work to restore balance, replanting forests not as a **corporate experiment**, but as an act of **atonement.**

Oxygen farms rise from the wreckage, bioengineered with humility rather than hubris—monitored, controlled, never left to spread unchecked.

Once-extinct plant species return, nurtured by

those who understand **now** what it means to play with life.

Those who **once denied the crisis now lead the restoration efforts.**

Those who **fought to expose the truth now guide the rebuilding.**

And **Zane Ortega**—the man once called a terrorist, a radical, a liar—**becomes something else.**

He **carries on Lillian's work**, not to create, but to **repair.**

He **teaches a new generation**, warning them of **unchecked ambition, of the arrogance that nearly cost humanity its breath.**

And for the first time, he is not fighting **against something.**

He is fighting **for something.**

A Tribute to the Lost & The Final Symbol of Hope

In what was once **the beating heart of a city**, a monument stands.

A sculpture of Lillian Kessler, hands outstretched, a shattered vial in one palm, a tiny sprout in the other.

Survivors leave flowers, notes, oxygen masks at its base—a quiet testament to the cost of both **destruction and redemption.**

Some **curse her name**, some **whisper their thanks**, but all know **her sacrifice saved them.**

And **far from the memorial**, in an abandoned street where no one watches—

A crack in the pavement.

A sliver of green.

A single **leaf, trembling in the wind.**

The first sign of life.

The Earth is healing.

Slowly.

Bloom & Decay *The Plant That Was Meant to Save the …

>Painfully.
>But surely.
>**Fade to black.**

www.ingramcontent.com/pod-product-compliance
Lightning Source LLC
LaVergne TN
LVHW020439080526
838202LV00055B/5269